SHERLOCK HOLMES

AND THE DISAPPEARING DIAMOND

SHERLOCK HOLMES

AND THE DISAPPEARING DIAMOND

SAM HEARN

SCHOLASTIC

Scholastic Children's Books
An imprint of Scholastic Ltd
Euston House, 24 Eversholt Street, London, NW1 1DB, UK
Registered office: Westfield Road, Southam, Warwickshire, CV47 0RA

First published in the UK by Scholastic Ltd, 2016

ISBN 978 1407 16184 6
C & F ISBN 978 1407 17294 1

A CIP catalogue record for this book
is available from the British Library.

Printed by CPI Group (UK) Ltd, Croydon, CR0 4YY
Papers used by Scholastic Children's Books are made
from wood grown in sustainable forests.

1 3 5 7 9 10 8 6 4 2

With special thanks to Sir Arthur Conan Doyle's literary estate for
permission to use the Sherlock Holmes characters.
www.scholastic.co.uk

For
EMILY
&
OUR
little
Missy
x

Yearbook

Meet the class ...

SHERLOCK HOLMES
Big brain or big-head? We'll see.

Most likely to ... who knows? He's such a mystery.

JOHN WATSON
The new kid in school. Loves writing, drawing, eating biscuits and drinking hot chocolate.

Most likely to ... be a doctor – maybe!

MARTHA HUDSON
A class leader. Funny and super confident.

Most likely to ... succeed at EVERYTHING!

JAMES MORIARTY
Sherlock's nemesis... He's annoying, selfish and always where you don't want him to be.

Most likely to ... take over the world.

MARTIN & HENRY BAKER
Twin brothers whose dad is a DI at Scotland Yard!

Most likely to ... follow in their father's footsteps and become a crime-fighting duo.

DAZ
Loses everything! Yes, everything.

Most likely to ... become a life coach (when he finally sorts himself out).

BART
John's old pal from primary school days. Fresh-faced, friendly and super cool.

Most likely to ... become a graphic designer.

MR GAPP
The coolest teacher in the school. Making learning fun since FOR EVER!

Most likely to ... go down in Baker Street history.

BASKERVILLE
The coolest doggy detective ever! He can sniff out a custard cream a mile off.

Most likely to ... get belly rubs.

London.

Somewhere off Baker Street.
Sherlock!
Sherlock!

Typical Sherlock. He's always a few steps ahead.
Keep up, Watson!

Always chasing the next lead.
WOOF!
I know, Baskerville
I'm going as fast as I can.

Where are we going anyway?
You'll see, Watson.
Trouble is, once Sherlock gets going, there's just no stopping him.
He's like a bloodhound on a scent!
I'm going where the clues lead...
Where the adventure takes us...
Now hurry up!
Well, I don't mind a bit of adventure. I mean, who would?
You better stay here, Baskerville.

I just had no idea how crazy it would be...

THE GAME IS AFOOT!

Or what sort of trouble we'd end up in...

Baker Street Academy
Encouraging excellence and nurturing talent

Baker Street Academ
Baker Street
London

Dear Mr and Mrs Watson,

We are very pleased to accept John into Baker Street Academy and look forward to welcoming him on Monday 8th. I'm delighted to enclose our latest prospectus, containing detailed information about our varied teaching programme and excellent range of extra-curricular activities. If there are any questions that you would like to ask, please don't hesitate to get in touch with me directly or through my assistant, Mrs Staveley.

In the meantime I would like to wish you well for your arrival back in London. I hope that your journey goes as smoothly as possible.

Mrs M. Cavendish

Mrs M. Cavendish,
Head Teacher
BA (Hons), MA

demy.
etropolitan

nd
cademy is the

aker Street
ts with
ities and
ur cap: from

chess clubs and board game groups to sporting activities and a range of musical and dramatic societies, Baker Street Academy is the very best place for students to find and fine-tune their interests and emerging talents.

First Year Academy Faculty:

Mrs Cavendish, Head Teacher
Mrs Staveley, Administrative Assistant
Mr Burlington, Deputy Head, English
Mr Mistry, Maths, IT
Mr Spice, Science, Technology
Ms DeRossi, History, Languages cover
Mrs Parker, Arts, Music
Mr Gapp, Languages
Mr Greenwood, Miss Jackson, PE

1

JOHN WATSON

Likes: reading, writing, doodling.
Wants to be a doctor. Maybe!

Adventure... Craziness... Trouble... It wasn't always like that though. At least not before I met Sherlock Homes, I mean. I should probably start somewhere near the beginning, otherwise this is going to get a bit confusing!

My name's John. John Watson. Yep, that's me up there with the glasses and the goofy grin. To be honest, my first day at Baker Street Academy was a bit nerve-wracking! I'd been away for what seemed like my whole life, and I could only remember little bits and pieces from the last time I was in London and going to a proper school like this... But, yep, there I was, the completely, obviously sticking-out "new boy" with no friends – totally nervous, a little bit excited and to make it even worse...

Ah! John Watson.
You're rather late.
We were expecting
you this morning.

Uh-oh! That's Mrs Cavendish, my new head teacher. She seemed pretty annoyed with me. It's probably not the best way to start my first day at a new school. Oops!

Beetroot red!

I went bright red and got all embarrassed, but luckily Mrs Cavendish got nicer pretty quickly. She must have felt sorry for me or something.

(Ms DeRossi)

Very Glamorous ↑

Mrs Cavendish introduced me to my new teacher, Ms DeRossi.

Then the secretary, Mrs Staveley, gave me some new workbooks to start me off in my studies. I thought Mrs Cavendish would send me straight to class after that, but instead she said that one of the other students was going to come and show me around a bit.

"Ah, Martha, there you are. This is our new arrival, John Watson. I thought you might like to show him the ropes a bit today as he gets settled in."

(This is Martha. Confident smile and mischievous eyes.)

Hi, John. Pleased to meet you!
Welcome to Baker Street Academy.

A good start, right? Yeah, I thought so too, but then she grinned cheekily and whispered, "Nice shade of red you've gone there!" Oh no. I'm doomed! This is going to be me every day for the rest of my life...

DOOMED →

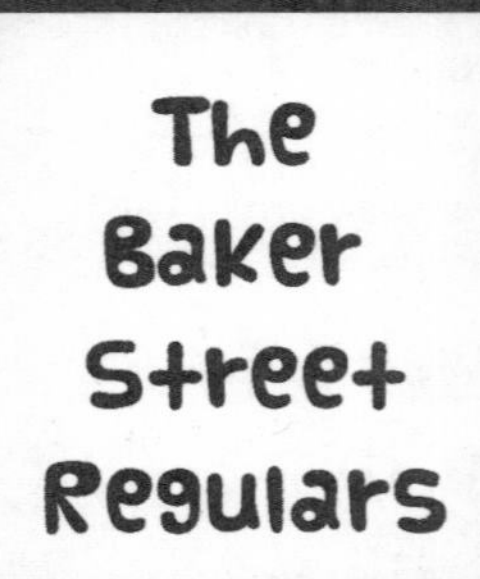
The Baker Street Regulars

Way to start your first day, John!
Don't they have alarm clocks where you come from? Hehe.

I know, I know. I've always had a bit of a lateness problem.

Mum's always joking that I was late for my own birth, so I'm probably double doomed. What can I say?

S'all right, John, I'm just messing with you. Come on, I'll take you to meet a good friend of mine.

Martha smiled and gave me a friendly nudge, then we strolled our way through the school corridors.

Hi, Martha!
Hi, Amber!
This is John. He's new.
Cool. Good to meet you, John!

"He's always losing stuff," whispered Martha as we passed them by. "It's so funny!"

Hey, Nisha! Hi, Ems!
Nah, I'll see you later.
I'm on new-kid duties. This is John.

Cool. See you later then.
Nice to meet you John!

Just then, a cool-looking teacher came out of a classroom in front of us.

Oh, hi, Mr Gapp. This is John. He's new here today.

Hello, Martha. Hello, John. Always nice to meet a new face at Baker Street Academy!
I'll look forward to seeing you in class, young man.

"Always pays to be on the good side of the teachers," added Martha as he walked away. "That's Mr Gapp – he's one of the best."

So Martha seems pretty cool! Even if she did like to make fun of me a bit! She's totally funny and super confident, and from what I can tell, she knows pretty much everybody in the whole school, even the teachers!

"Hey, there's Bart," Martha pointed at a fresh-faced boy heading our way. "Hi, Bart, this is John."

Oh, wow. Talk about weird! I can't believe I (literally) bumped into somebody at school that I knew already! Bart was one of my best friends from when I was young. Martha really does know everybody!

Bart! Wow, that's amazing. I haven't seen you since we were at Stamford Primary.
Yeah! That's a long story...

I know! It's crazy! Where have you been then, John? My mum said you'd moved away.

Mum and Dad are doctors. Dad works in the armed forces, so we've moved around a lot! We've lived in all sorts of places – England, Scotland, Germany, Spain – I don't remember all of them though. I was probably too young. I've just been in the Middle East, 'cos Dad was out in Afghanistan.

Wow! Cool. So now you're the new boy then?
Yep. 'Fraid so!
SHERLOCK?

You'll like it here. It's pretty good fun at Baker Street Academy. Hey – talking of fun, have you met Sherlock yet?
Ha ha! Exactly! You should see what's happening in the science room... Catch you guys later.

Ha! No, he hasn't. I'm saving the best bit till last.

"Who's Sherlock?" I asked as we left Bart and carried on to wherever it was Martha was taking me.

He's the good friend of mine I mentioned – you'll like him! Come on!
Ahh. There's a good boy! There's a good good boy. Come on, Mr Furry Pants! Who's a Mr Fluffy Trousers then?

Yeah, I know... I thought Martha was talking to me there for a minute as well. But it turns out that the school even has a dog! How cool is that?!

THIS IS BASKERVILLE

Martha said he belongs to the caretaker, Mr Musgrave, and his wife, but he's allowed to go pretty much wherever he wants by the looks of it! Martha said she gets to take him for walks sometimes too.

WOOF!
WOOF!

We gave him a good fuss for a few minutes until he ran off woofing after some other dog adventure, then Martha took me along to the science block to meet this mysterious friend of hers...

We'd barely got through the classroom door when a voice called out from the far side of the room...

Martha!
You're just in time.
ROOM 39
SCIENCE
MR SPICE

2 SHERLOCK GIVES A DEMONSTRATION

Hi, Sherlock. Just in time for what?

That's exactly what I was thinking... As we walked into the science room I could barely see a thing, there was so much smoke and mist everywhere. An excited face appeared out of the haze and then the boy that it belonged to came running towards us waving a test tube in his hand.

For this! I've done it.
It's the perfect result.
Oh, I see you've brought a friend with you...
"Yes! Sherlock, this is J—"

No, wait! Don't tell me. J ... James ... no, John ... Watson. Yes! How are you, John?
I'm all right, thanks.
Wait, hang on a minute – how did you know my name?!
Ha! Never mind that. It's obvious.

Sherlock was smiling and looking me up and down like I was another science experiment.

You had a long flight yesterday, I take it? Mmm-hmm. Plenty of time for writing and drawing in your journal. Had a bit of trouble finding us too, I see - the roadworks, I suppose. No wonder you were late today!

So this is Sherlock, I thought to myself... Martha's good friend and possibly some sort of super-brained mind reader! Something weird was going on here... Better just try to play it cool.

"Er ... yeah. Nice to meet you, Sherlock. Is that ... blood?"

I pointed to the test tube he was clutching. It had some suspicious dark crimson liquid in it. Sherlock's face lit up and he burst out laughing.

Ha ha! Blood! It's mostly raspberry, John. That and a few other special ingredients. I've been working on the perfect base for an ice-cold treat. A bit of help from Mr Spice's chemistry supplies and I'd say you won't find a better smoothie this side of Oxford Street! Would you like to try?

Martha started laughing too. That explained the room full of mist then! I wondered if this was what Martha meant when she said she was saving the best bit till last.

"No, thanks," I said nervously. "I've already had my breakfast."

Ah. Well, never mind.

Sherlock smiled, put the test tube down on the desk nearby and brushed his hands off.

Hot chocolate's more your thing, I see. Yes. And croissants. You've had two already this morning! Almond and chocolate.

As the three of us made our way out of the classroom, Martha turned to me with a cheeky grin on her face.

"Biscuits eh? Baskerville's gonna like you, that's for sure. Ha ha!"

What can you say about that then? Talk about

GOBSMACKED.

I have absolutely no idea what just happened, but it was pretty amazing. I mean, how could he possibly have known any of that stuff? Martha just shrugged and said,

Don't worry about it, John. He's always like that. You'll get used to it.

I suppose I will! Martha seems to like him a lot anyway. Still, it was a bit strange – although not the strangest thing to happen on my first day. Meeting Sherlock might have been weird, but at least it was fun – which is more than I can say for bumping into

out in the hall...

JAMES MORIARTY

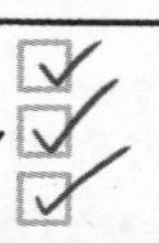
SMARMY GRIN
EVIL EYEBROWS
BAD ATTITUDE

WELL, WELL. LOOK WHO IT IS. FOUND A NEW PET HAVE YOU, SHERLOCK?
THERE'S A GOOD DOGGY. HERE, BOY!

Yeah, I know, I thought he was talking to Baskerville too! No such luck. He doesn't seem too nice, this guy. His friends didn't look much nicer either.

Ugh! Shut up, James. Just ignore him, John. He thinks he's so clever.

CLEVERER THAN YOU, MARTHA. BUT THAT'S NOT SO HARD.
CATCH YOU LATER, KIDDIES. SHERLOCK.

"What was that all about?" I asked.

"James Moriarty," replied Sherlock as James and his cronies sloped off. "Don't worry about him. I think he likes you though, Martha."

Martha gave Sherlock a nudge. "Yuck. No thanks! I wish he'd go back to that fancy-pants junior school in America or wherever it was that he transferred from."

"I take it he's not a friend then," I said.

"It's elementary, Martha," said Sherlock.

Martha looked as confused as I felt.

What's elementary?
They call it "elementary school" in America.
Besides, he was at an international school in Switzerland. Near his family home in Reichenbach Falls. You really should pay more attention.
Right - lunch time?
Smarty pants!

It turns out starting a new school wasn't so bad after all, even if meeting the head teacher was a bit scary – and not exactly **everybody** was friendly...

The rest of the day went by in a blur, with so many new names and faces to take in.

I reckon I got on all right though. I'm looking forward to the art classes. English too.

My class teacher, **Ms DeRossi**, seems really nice. She's from Italy and is new this year as well, so we have that in common.

She teaches history, and **Martha** and **Sherlock** said we'll be going on a school trip to a **MUSEUM** for our Victorian history project soon.

Maybe I'll ask them about it later... **OH YEAH!**

I almost forgot. **Martha's** invited me over to her house after school with **Sherlock**, which should be cool!

Looks like **Bart** was right: I think I'm going to like it here.

221B
3

Wow! Look at all this stuff. This is so cool. Clothes, chairs, books, papers!
Look, I've found a pipe. And a stinky old slipper.
Yuck – it's filled with some nasty brown stuff! Weird.
That's tobacco, John.
I've got hats! And more books. Hmm ... very interesting.
There's an old violin over here. And some test tubes in a box.
Ooh, and a cape – I've always wanted one of these!
Now that would definitely look much better on me!

Martha's house is **AMAZING**. She and her mum, Mrs Hudson, live near the school at 221B Baker Street.

It's one of those old London houses with railings outside and it's got four floors! I've never even been in a house like it before.

When Martha told her mum we were doing a history project on the Victorians, she said we should take a look in the old top-floor rooms upstairs. She wasn't wrong! It's like nobody has decorated them for about a hundred years.

Each one has still got its own little fireplace and really creaky old floorboards. The rooms are pretty small though, especially as they're filled with all this old stuff in boxes. Apparently the people who lived in this house even had servants and maids. Can you believe that? Life used to be very different!

tuff there is," I said

t was like being in a

. "It's amazing."

tha. "I didn't know it was even

that there have been lodgers

ctorian times, so hopefully there

wil ff here for our project."

"That'd be brilliant!" I said.

We found all sorts of interesting things; some useful things; some odd things; and some gross things. Like bedpans – yuck! (Imagine having to go to the toilet in a bowl and stick it back under your bed all night long. No, thanks!) We carried on rummaging around for ages – it was great fun.

A VICTORIAN DETECTIVE AND A PROBLEM

"Look," I said. "Another hat! It looks a bit stupid. I can't tell if that's the front or the back."

That's called a deerstalker. And it's a nice little problem for you. What can you tell me about it?

I stared at the hat to see if anything came to mind. "I don't know... Whoever wore it had a massive big head, that's the first thing I can tell. A big head and cold ears. Ha ha!"

Oh, come on, John, you're not really trying.

Sherlock swiped the hat from me and started examining it.

Let me see. Hmm... I'd say he was a man of distinction. A man with a sharp mind and a strong character. I'd say he had a considerable intellect too. A man who could easily match the highest intelligence or the very lowest wit - and, what's more, he was a formidable problem-solver. Not to mention a man of action, when needed. Yes, he was most likely a brilliant detective. His name was ... Sherinford.

And by the looks of it, I'd say he smoked this pipe, wore this cape and played the violin too!

Wow! Sherlock, you got all that from just looking at the hat? That's amazing!

Not really, John. It's obvious. You saw it all yourself, but you just weren't looking properly.

OH MY GOD.
You are such a big head!

Ha ha! It's all right, Martha, I'm just having a bit of fun! The name tag in the hat says "Sherinford". The size of the hat implies a man with a large brain. Discolouration along the rim shows that he was a smoker, and the fact that it's slightly worn on one side implies that he had a violin on his shoulder. And the material matches the cape, showing that they would be worn together.

"How did you know he was a detective?" I asked.

Sherlock turned his attention back to the pile he'd just been investigating. "I was reading through these old journals and bits of paper whilst you two were rummaging around over there. There's some illustrated stories written about his cases. Pretty impressive stuff from the look of it."

"Speaking of big heads, what's the story with James Moriarty?" I asked Sherlock. I figured now was as good a time as any to ask.

"What isn't the story with Moriarty, I should say, John! He is exactly what he seems to be: annoying, selfish and always where you don't want him to be. A bit like a bad smell, lingering around and getting up your nose. Do you know what I mean?"

"Erm. Sort of, yeah," I said, looking over at Martha, who was rolling her eyes. "I thought he was rude. And he certainly seemed to think he was pretty clever."

"He is clever, John," said Sherlock, sounding a bit muffled as he worked his way under another dust sheet. "And definitely rude. Wherever trouble is, James is probably not far away. You might even call him my nemesis. He's a shadow in the shade, the unseen reflection in the mirror, the twisted words you never..."

Yep. I sort of switched off a bit here. I just carried on smiling and let Sherlock waffle. Martha said he does that all the time, especially when it comes to Moriarty.

We carried on rummaging around upstairs for ages after that, and then Mrs Hudson made us some snacks. It was great fun. Probably the best day I've had in a long time.

After-School Clubs

Baker Street Academy News Team Needs **YOU!**

Are you a budding writer? Do you have an investigative mind? Do you know which way to point a camera? If the answer is YES to any of these questions, why not get involved with the Baker Street Academy news team? First meeting on Tuesday lunchtime in the music room.

Class 2 Visit to the B&A Museum

All students attending the Victorian history trip to the B&A Museum must have their signed permission slips returned by the end of the month. Don't forget to hand them in to Ms DeRossi ASAP!

Maths! English! Languages! Science!

Sign up now for extra tuition on your chosen subject.

BASKERVILLE!

HOW TO SOLVE A PROBLEM LIKE SHERLOCK!

So I think I'm settling in at Baker Street Academy now. A few weeks have gone by and I'm getting to know everybody a bit better. I really like Martha and she and Sherlock hang out a lot together, so I'm getting to know him too. I don't know how to describe him as I've never met anybody quite like him! He's definitely a bit weird (and it's not just me who thinks that). For instance, he knows loads about:

- Science and chemistry – he knows more than Mr Spice, who even lets him work on his own experiments.

- Anatomy – it's like he knows a skeleton inside out!

- Geology – he knows all about soils and types of rock and where particular plants grow.

- Geography – Martha reckons he knows his way around all of London, without ever needing to think twice about where something is!

But he doesn't know anything about:

- Planets and space, even basic stuff like the earth spinning around the sun or that we might go to Mars one day.

- Popular culture – ask him about the latest movies or books and he just looks blank.

I asked him about it one day and he said, "The thing is, John, my brain's like Martha's attic: there's only just enough room to keep filling it with the best things!"

He's amazing at problem-solving too. He finished the hardest maths test I've ever done in under five minutes. (I could tell Moriarty was annoyed – he's really good too). He guessed the combination on Darren's locker without even looking. And there was the time he worked out where one of the Baker Boys' missing phone was. He said he'd solved it just by observing how long it had taken for the bananas in the canteen to start going brown...!? I wrote it all down in my journal and called it "The Case of the Speckled Banana".

As you can probably tell, Sherlock can be a bit funny-sounding at times too, although maybe that's not surprising when I look at some of the things he likes to read...

Sometimes if there are no problems to be solved he gets really grumpy and says stuff like:

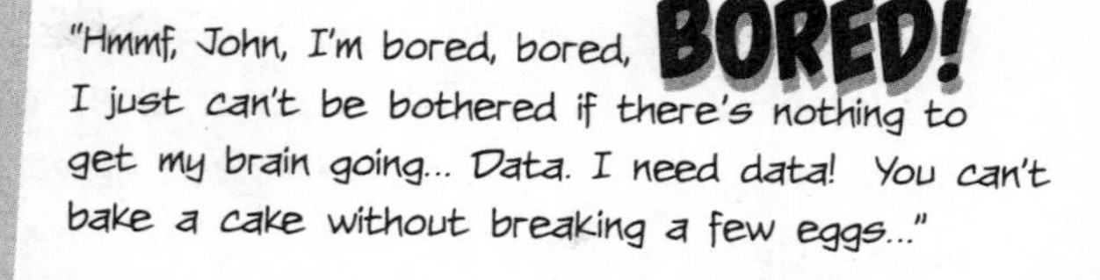

"Hmmf, John, I'm bored, bored, BORED!
I just can't be bothered if there's nothing to get my brain going... Data. I need data! You can't bake a cake without breaking a few eggs..."

And sometimes when he is in the middle of a problem he gets really excited and words come out of his mouth so fast, it sounds like gibberish:

"I can't help it, I'm afraid, John. I'm interested in things! Things that other people aren't looking for: small things, big things, irrelevant things, trifles. Pancakes! It's all in the details. Once you start looking at something, even the smallest, strangest and most ridiculous thing can often lead you to the truth. John? John! Watson! Give me your iPad!"

Oh yeah, my iPad... My mum and dad gave it to me as a present so that I could write my stories on it and keep all my pictures together. Sherlock didn't give it back for a whole day. He's always doing things like that. It can be a bit annoying! I suppose it's all part of what makes Sherlock Holmes who he is though, and why Baker Street Academy is such an exciting place to be.

Hey, are you going to try and do something for the school newspaper this year, Martha?
Yeah! I reckon we should probably take some pictures again. We got some really good ones last year.
Brilliant idea! What about you, John? You're always writing or scribbling things.
Maybe I could do a school blog? I was thinking about writing some funny short stories. I could even illustrate them a bit.
You mean, like a comic? About the school?
Yeah, definitely! I might even try and get Baskerville in there too. He's the coolest dog ever.
WOOF!
Cheekiest dog ever, you mean. Haha!

TAPPY
TAP
TAP
TAP
TAP
TAPPY
TAP
TAP
TAP
TAP
TAP
TAP
TAP
TAP TAPPY TAP
TAP

Baker Street A..

https://www.bakerstreetbloggers.blogsplodge.com/2016/10/baker-s

Baker Street Academy Blog

Monday 3rd

Cool news! The school news team love my idea for a Baker Street Academy Blog. I'm going to have a go at writing some funny stories and comics for it – there's so much going on it's given me plenty of ideas...

 0 Comments

Museum Visit

Tuesday 4th

OK, Baker Street Blog readers! We have our first announcement! As you all know, our class history topic this year is the Victorians, and to start things off in style there is going to be a class outing to the British Arts & Antiquities Museum (B&A). You'll need to remember to bring your worksheets, notebooks, pencil cases and sense of Victorian adventure! I can't wait!

 1 Comment

Comments:

Ms DeRossi: Thanks, John! Mr Gapp and I are very much looking forward to the trip. We'll be spending the morning doing some research on the Victorian period and looking at the many artefacts on display at the museum, so you should all get some good ideas for your class projects. And if there's time we'll try to fit in a special surprise exhibit in the afternoon too!

3 hours ago

4
ADVENTURE AT THE MUSEUM
OK, class, gather round. Make sure you all stick together now. Mr Gapp, do you want to do a quick headcount?
Sure thing, Ms DeRossi. Thumbs up - all present and accounted for! OK, gang, let's go upstairs.

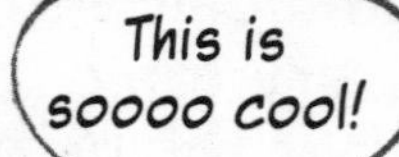
This is soooo cool!

B&A
-EXPLORE THE
25 TREASUR
I wanna see the 25 Treasures exhibition!
Yeah, me too!

I wanna see the big statues!
I want to see all the old armour and stuff.
I want to see the old clothes and costumes!
NEED A NEW OUTFIT, DO YOU? HA HA!

Do we really have to
o and look at all the
Victorian stuff?
BORING!

OK, OK. Calm down, everybody. We're going to see as much as we can! We've got all day and it's going to be great.

OH! MI SCUSI – AHEM! EXCUSE ME, MADAM. I'M TERRIBLY SORRY.
BUMP!

Interesting, isn't it, Watson?

Sherlock! Where've you been?
I thought you'd disappeared.

I've been doing a spot of people watching, John. A fascinating hobby, don't you think? And sometimes most enlightening...

Well, I'm not exactly sure what Sherlock was finding so interesting, but – wow! The museum is amazing. And massive! There's stuff from all over the world: Ancient Rome, China, the Middle East and Ancient Greece too. There are gold Buddhas and trinkets and treasures and jewels and rooms full of paintings and – oh man, I'm talking about GIANT paintings. There's even great big bits of old buildings... It's incredible! And all of this before we even started to look at things for our school project. I could probably come here every week and still not get through it all.

Although you can't always please everybody...

"Oh my god. This is **SO** boring!" complained Martha after about five minutes. "Who wants to look at a load of old teapots all day? If it's not that, it's portraits of posh ladies, stuck-up gents and fancy dogs... Ooh, hang on a minute... Now that's more like it!"

NICK-NACKS & MUGSHOTS

Finally we reached the Victorian display. The Victorians had some cool stuff all right, even if it was a bit strange. It's like they had a little gadget for everything they could think of: combs and brushes and mirrors, and all sorts of weird clips and fasteners, buttons and brooches and silly suspenders on your clothes.

There was plenty of interesting stuff for our school projects – lots about the British Empire and how far it stretched across the world, and lots of Victorian inventions and buildings. We even got to try on some clothes.

Hey, these look a bit like some of the things we found in your house, Martha.
Yeah, they've got more of those funny hats and a cape too.
Oops! This one's a bit big...
Nice, John. You look very Victorian. All you need now is a moustache! Haha!

Hey, look at these nifty old cameras!

Martha had found a display cabinet full of old-fashioned cameras. That's another thing the Victorians invented. "They took a lot of photos, didn't they?" she said, as she got out her phone and held it up, ready to snap a picture.

"Yes. No selfies though, Martha!" said Sherlock from across the room. He was staring up at a huge glass cabinet filled with pictures of some scary, grizzled-looking people. "Come and look at these."

Very funny, Sherlock. Who are this lot then?
They're criminals. Victorian London's most vicious and vile. Deadly to the very last.
They look horrible! What's wrong with their faces?

Well, that's one more strange thing about the Victorians. All these photos were taken as memento mori
M-Minty what-what?
Memento mori. It means they were dead.
What?! Eurgh!

I think we were pretty happy to leave the Victorians behind after that!

TREASURE HUNT

The morning sped by and soon it was time for our surprise – talk about saving the best till last! Ms DeRossi and Mr Gapp handed out maps for the 25 Treasures exhibition. Man, it was so cool! It was like a massive treasure hunt of all the most unusual and special objects in the museum. We went round trying to see who could spot them first. I was with Sherlock and Martha, Darren was with Martin and Henry, Bart was with Em and Nisha and a few others were off with Mr Gapp. James Moriarty was with his cronies, Seb and Charlie. As usual it didn't take them long to start spoiling the atmosphere...

But I wasn't going to let them bother me – there was just so much to see.

There was an amazing room with humungous marble statues, and what looked like a golden doorway to a magical land.

An incredible notebook belonging to Leonardo da Vinci, and an original book of Shakespeare's plays.

A ginormous four-poster bed and what looked like a huge flying carpet, and a man-eating tiger! Not to mention the most famous diamond known to humanity,

THE ALPINE STAR...

OH MY GOD, did you see the Alpine Star? I'm not one for glitz but it's amazing. I've never seen anything like it. I wouldn't mind owning that.
Ugh! I wasn't talking to you, thanks.
What would you know, James? You're just jealous. I bet you wish you had a diamond like that.
Ha ha. Fat chance!
HA! YOU KNOW MOST OF THIS STUFF ACTUALLY BELONGS TO OTHER PEOPLE, RIGHT? IT'S ALL JUST STOLEN GOODS.
OH, PLEASE. MY FAMILY COULD BUY THIS MUSEUM – AND YOURS LIVE IN ONE! HUR HUR!

The Alpine Star WAS amazing - Martha was raving about it. I couldn't believe how sparkly it was. But Sherlock kept wandering off - he wasn't really that bothered by all the cool stuff on display. He seemed more interested in the museum staff than anything else. He kept staring at all the different staff members walking around, a thoughtful look on his face.

All too soon it was time to leave, and we hadn't finished the treasure hunt. I did manage half a drawing of a really cool statue of Emperor Napoleon wearing a hat though! Oh well – it's a good excuse to come back!

But just as we were getting ready to leave, everything went weird. I mean, I say weird – but I mean WEIRD – like totally, absolutely freakishly crazy weird...

5 THE SCIENCE OF DISTRACTION

The first thing I knew, music started playing in the gallery below us...

It was so loud, like, just blasting out all of a sudden. Martha's friends got excited because it was their favourite track,

UPTOWN FUNKY!

It was crazy! All of a sudden a massive crowd of what looked like museum staff flooded into the room...

Wait a minute, what are all those people doing?

Are they museum staff?

I think they're just dressed up as staff. This is so weird!

Look – they're dancing!

WOAH!

Hey, Ms DeRossi, check it out. It's a flash mob!

I'd seen videos of this kind of stuff before, but it's different when it happens right next to you. At first we all thought it was great fun. Daz and a couple of the girls even started to join in. It was brilliant!

Just then...

BEEEEEEEEP BEEEEEEEEP

BEEEEEEEEP BEEEEEEEEP

BEEEEEEEEP BEEEEEEEEP

BEEEEEEEEP BEEEEEEEEP

BEEEEEEEEP BEEEEEEEEP

BEEEEEEEEP BEEEEEEEEP

The alarms started going off – and I knew that wasn't a good sound, especially when I heard shouting and smashing noises in the background.

What's going on?!
Secret spies on a mission?
NINJAS!
Nope, definitely spies...

People were running everywhere, trying to get out of the way.

"OK, everybody, stay together. Quickly, now – we need to make our way out of the building. Everybody follow me," cried Martha.

"Where's Sherlock? And where's Ms DeRossi?" I yelled.

"Look, there's Mr Gapp and the others – let's join them," Martha said.

"Wait a minute – is that the police?"

"Yeah... Hey, that's my dad!" shouted Henry.

"Whoah! This is AWESOME! So much for a boring trip to the museum..."

FLASH ROB!

The British Arts & Antiquities Museum in West London saw the most extraordinary scenes earlier today as it was momentarily overtaken by what can only be described as a FLASH MOB ROBBERY ATTEMPT! Hundreds of visitors, including children on a school trip, were stunned as a crowd dressed in museum staff uniforms caused just enough of a distraction to enable a canny thief to make a smash and grab of the PRICELESS Alpine Star, a jewel with a long and troubled history.

The jewel was on display as part of the 25 Treasures exhibition. After touring European arts venues for the last few years, the collection of exhibits has only recently returned to their home at the B&A Museum…

More on page 4

Blue Car Bungle!

▶ Museum thief fails in ridiculous getaway attempt

by Benedict Cabbagebat

Bizarre goings-on at the B&A Museum led to some red-faced embarrassment for a NOT-so-light-fingered thief who attempted to steal a famous jewel in broad daylight. After making off with the famous Alpine Star gem during a flash mob event, things turned sour for the criminal when he made his getaway.

Red-Handed: Pietro Vencini

The thief, a 43-year-old Italian national named Pietro Vencini, made his getaway in an ancient blue Fiat 500, but barely made it a few hundred metres down the road through the London traffic before spluttering to a stop. The police, led by

D.I. Hero: Adrian Baker

Detective Inspector Adrian Baker of Scotland Yard, were able to apprehend him within minutes to the cheers of watching crowds.

The suspect had been working as a staff member at the B&A Museum for the past three weeks before making his attempt. His lawyer has released a brief statement:

"*My client has been the victim of a terrible injustice. We will be cooperating fully with the police as we work towards clearing his name. Pietro is a kind-hearted family man. He is greatly missing his son, Napoleon. Everything points to him being an upstanding pillar of the community. He is hoping to be able to return to his job at the museum shortly.*"

Arts Online: Ne..

https://www.artsonline.co.uk/news-museums-london-b&a-robbery-or

 Arts Online 

News > Museums > London

THE ALPINE STAR

The British Arts & Antiquities Museum has had more than its fair share of time in the spotlight over the 150 years since its founding. No event this century, however, can match the excitement and intrigue sparked by the return of the 25 Treasures exhibition to its spiritual home … particularly the mysterious Alpine Star, which has once again hit the news this week as the object of an outrageous attempted theft.

The Alpine Star was discovered in the nineteenth century, and since then its origins have been hotly debated. Taken from an Indian mine during an expedition, it is said to be cursed.

At the time of writing, the Alpine Star is safely back in the museum's collection, and will be shown in a temporary display, pending an independent security review and ongoing police investigations.

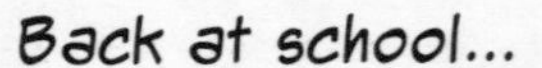

OH MY GOD.

Did you hear about what happened at the museum?

Yeah, of course! Everyone's been messaging about it!

Ms DeRossi's class were there when it happened.

I saw Sherlock on TV!

Yeah, and the Baker Boys' dad too!

Shut up!?

Oh, WOW. Baker Street Academy is gonna be famous!

Someone told me James Moriarty knows who did it...

My dad says the police knew what was going on already. They always do.

BUT ... BUT ... BUT, DAD...

I'M SORRY. I'LL MAKE IT UP TO YOU, I PROMISE.

BUT WHY? I WANT TO HELP.

I CAN FIND IT. I KNOW I CAN! YOU'LL SEE.

OK. I'M SORRY. IT WON'T HAPPEN AGAIN.

YES. BYE, DAD.

Wow. School was unbelievably crazy this week. Pretty much everyone was talking about the Alpine Star and what happened when our class was at the museum.

It's not every day you're right slap-bang in the middle of a jewel theft gone wrong...

Apparently Ms DeRossi and Mr Gapp even had to be interviewed by the police – and someone said that Martin and Henry's dad, Inspector Baker, would be coming into school soon to speak to the whole class too. Double crazy!

"So where did you get to when all the craziness started?" I asked Sherlock, when the three of us finally had a minute alone . "I didn't see you once the alarms went off."

"Yeah, you did your disappearing act again, didn't you?" added Martha, rolling her eyes.

"I was there, John, don't worry. Just following my own line of enquiry. As it happens, I had a message from my brother Mycroft the day before. It seems he had a suspicion that something interesting would be happening at the museum besides our little school visit!"

Tut. Sherlock and his surprises as usual. I didn't even know he had a brother. And I'm sorry but Mycroft? What was with the weird names? It wouldn't surprise me if he was some sort of spy or something!

"Oh, Mycroft's really nice, John," Martha pointed out helpfully. "He's loads older than us. Mum really likes him too! Sherlock lives with him."

"Yes, yes, Martha. I'm sure John'll meet him at some point. Anyway, Mycroft sent me a message warning me that something might go down whilst we were at the museum, so I decided to keep a close eye on what was going on. The first thing I noticed was that there were a lot of extra museum staff around, one of whom I thought was particularly interesting. After everything started getting a bit... musical, I noticed that one of the fire exit doors had been left open – so I slipped through just to have a look..."

Wow, I thought to myself. This was not the sort of day that I'd been having at the museum! Trust Sherlock to be that curious.

"But then just a few moments later I realized I wasn't alone. The door opened at the other end of the corridor I found myself in, and if I'm not mistaken, the man who came through it was our very own Alpine Star thief - clutching the jewel itself!"

WHAT! YOU SAW THE THIEF!? BEFORE THE POLICE GOT HIM?!

Incredible! I just can't believe how mad everything has gone in the last few days. Weird flash mobs, an attempted jewel theft, secret messages... And Sherlock saw the thief with his own eyes!

And all because of a fancy old Victorian jewel!

"Ah. But what a jewel, Martha. It was magnificent! When you see it as the light catches it, as I did in the corridor ... it's absolutely brilliant. It transports you to a different world..."

For many decades, the Alpine Star was the largest diamond known to man. In Victorian times it was considered one of the earth's rarest treasures. Discovered in the Beeton Mine in 1887, the largest cut of the Great Indian White Diamond, it quickly made its way to Europe - although many say that it would have been better if it had never been found in the first place, considering the misery and misfortune that have fallen on those who have claimed ownership of it through the years.

"Eh? Sherlock, how do you know all this stuff?"

"I've done my research – and I found this helpful leaflet. Well, I think we can find the time for another little visit to the museum to see the Alpine Star restored to its rightful place. I've a sparkling suspicion that there's more going on here than meets the eye..."

BASKERVILLE!

SPOTTED

Wait a minute. What's that cheeky-but-loveable hound Baskerville been up to this time?!

Reports have come in that Baskerville was seen this morning looking very pleased with himself indeed, carrying what can only be described as a STINKY SPORTS SOCK.

Hey! That's mine!

Oops! This is Darren. Oh dear, Dazzer. Losing stuff again, eh?

My mum's gonna go nuts. It was clean when I brought it to school... Anyone wanna do a swap?

Ooh, not likely, Darren. Perhaps our furry friend will bring you a replacement, if he finds a way into the changing room again!

Oh, that Baskerville!

Join us next time for another instalment of canine fun and games...

7 MORE THAN MEETS THE EYE

So Sherlock, Martha and I arranged to meet at the B&A again that weekend. I was pretty excited to be back at the museum, even if Martha had said it would be too much like schoolwork. Not for me, though. I knew that Sherlock was up to something and I wanted to find out what.

Martha was running a bit late, so Sherlock and I headed straight into the museum. After all the attention it had been getting recently, the galleries were buzzing with people, and I almost got lost in the crowds trying to keep up with Sherlock as he dashed all over the place. I couldn't seem to shake the feeling that Sherlock was planning more than just another fun day out...

What's going on, Sherlock? Why are we skulking around like a couple of extra museum thieves? I thought we came here to look at the Alpine Star.
We're just following up on something first, John. And as I suspected, we're not the only ones...

With that Moriarty melted into the throng of tourists. He really isn't very nice, is he? Actually it wouldn't surprise me if Sherlock had known all along that James was going to be at the museum today – he usually seems to know everything.

And then, a few minutes later we spotted Ms DeRossi too, hurrying through the crowd. It was like museum club or something! Sherlock insisted we didn't let Ms DeRossi spot us. I don't know why we couldn't just go and say hello.

Just then Martha arrived and we told her who we'd seen.

"One thing's for sure," grinned Martha, "she definitely seems to like history!"

"Well, she is a history teacher," I pointed out.

Luckily, Sherlock had decided that we could finally go and see the famous jewel. We picked up the 25 Treasures trail where we'd left off on our visit and worked our way through it until we got to the Alpine Star.

"Wow, look at it," cooed Martha. "It's even more beautiful than I remembered."

The three of us stood in front of the diamond. I had my nose totally squashed up against the glass cabinet (which you're not meant to do, by the way). There it was, all lit-up and sparkling. It looked pretty impressive.

"It's amazing!" I said.

"You're right. It is amazing, John," replied Sherlock with a mischievous grin on his face.

"Yeah, right," scoffed Martha, sarcastically. "What, are you a jewel expert now?"

"In a manner of speaking, yes. But there's no time for chat – the game is on!"

And before I could get in a "What are you talking about?" and a "What do you mean it's a fake?" Sherlock was marching off out of the room.

MAJOR MUCK-UP AT MUSEUM

We're going live now to our reporter outside the B&A Museum in London...

From bizarre bunglings to blatant porky-pies, comedy has turned to outrage at London's most famous museum this week.

After the blundering theft attempt made by Pietro Vencini last week, it seems the B&A Museum's curators must now share the embarrassment as the press are told that their Alpine Star attraction is actually a fake!

We spoke to some visitors soon after the discovery was announced.

Terry Raymond, 72, from West London, said: "Even I said it didn't look like much of a special diamond to me, didn't I, Barbs?"

"You did, Terry," said Barbara Raymond.

"You said it looked like a bit of old plastic."

And a bit of old plastic is in fact all it is.

What's next for the B&A Museum, we must wonder. News that a Shakespeare play has actually been written in gel pen on tea-stained paper?

Back to you in the studio...

Many thanks. Police have declined to comment at this stage in the inquiry but we have had a statement from the representative of the suspect currently being detained for attempted theft:

"I refer you to our earlier statement:

My client, Pietro Vencini, is a kind-hearted family man and an upstanding pillar of the community.

We are co-operating fully with the police and he is very much hoping to be able to return again to the museum. Thank you."

FORCE FIND FAKE

by Benedict Cabbagebat

Once again the British Arts & Antiquities Museum hits the news as, in an INCREDIBLE TWIST, it was revealed to the press that the Alpine Star jewel – one of the main attractions in the current 25 Treasures exhibition – is nothing more than a remarkable fake!

A diamond-authentication expert noticed that not all was as it seemed during the planned security review, following last week's infamous "Flash Rob" incident. Just what this means for the 25 Treasures exhibition and the museum's vast and up-till-now highly respected collections is yet to be seen…

Arts Online: Ne..

https://www.artsonline.co.uk/news-museums-london-b&a-robbery-c

Arts Online

News > Museums > London

MUSEUM MYSTERY

Confusion and speculation has followed the most recent revelation from the B&A museum that the recovered Alpine Star gemstone is actually nothing more than a highly skilled fake.

The discovery was only made after a bungled jewel theft earlier in the week.

The museum's director, Mr Humphrey Huffington, was quick to issue a statement:

"On behalf of the British Arts & Antiquities Museum I would like to say that this institution has never knowingly deceived the Great British public by exhibiting any object that is a fake or a forgery. Needless to say, we are as stunned as everyone else. It is our belief that the real gem was swapped during the attempted robbery."

So if Humphrey Huffington is correct and the real gem was swapped during the "robbery", the question is – where is the Alpine Star?

Whoa! Three guesses what everybody was talking about back at school. I just can't believe it. Not so long ago I was just your average, ordinary everyday kid, with his nose in a book or a pencil in his hand, making up stories – but fast-forward to Baker Street Academy and bang! No need to invent stories any more – it seems like every day a new one is beginning...

I tried to get some answers from Sherlock.

"John." Martha was looking at me with one of those looks on her face. "I think Sherlock's head is big enough already."

It's just so-

John.

But it's just so clever!

Really? I thought it was rather obvious myself.

"But what happens now then?" I babbled on. "I mean, do you think the real jewel is still out there somewhere? It could've been missing for years! Do you think we'll be able to find it?"

Yes. Presumably. I doubt it. I should think so. That's a lot of questions, Watson. It's definitely an LPP.

Yeah. Definitely. Um - What?

In fact I'd go so far as to say it was a three LPP.

What's an LPP?

A liquorice pipe problem, John! Here. You should try one.

BANNISTER'S
OLDE
FASHIONED
LIQUORIC
flavoured
CONFECTION
PIPES
A NOVELTY TREAT!

Yuck! I did try one. It was **DISGUSTING.**

I don't think anybody got much work done that day. In class people were coming up with all kinds of crazy ideas about the Alpine Star, and for some reason James was in a worse mood than usual all day long.

Ms DeRossi looked distracted, like she had other things on her mind. I'm sure that's the only reason we didn't all end up in detention!

I'm going round Martha's later with Sherlock so maybe we can pick his brains a bit more about where the Alpine Star might be. One thing's for sure, all this is giving me some great ideas for stories...

THE HOUND CALLED BASKERVILLE
8

Dear reader – here is mystery! Spines will tingle and bones will be chilled! Dear reader, here is adventure! It is with you at every turn! Be sure that no one is following you, and watch where you are stepping! And, dear reader, here is excitement! Yes, indeed. Heart-pounding, brain-busting, mind-meddling excitement.

But what does it all mean? What is mystery without a set of clues? What is adventure, without the adventurer? And what is a problem without a solution? The answer can only be found by the most amazing, the most astounding, the most extraordinary companion a person could have. Why, it's none other than our four-legged friend. Wait for it now, dear reader...

Yes, here he comes...

IT'S BASKERVILLE THE WONDER DOG!

Catching crime firmly in his jaws. ***GRRR!***

Sniffing out suspicion!
WOOF!

Doggedly detecting
the dastardly villain,
who can only be
named as...

Oh really, John. Don't you think you're getting a bit too theatrical? I know you just can't stop yourself, but it might help if you stuck to the facts!

Hey! I'm just having bit of fun, Sherlock. Anyway, I can't help it. It's all so exciting! And weird!

I just wanted to get some of the craziness out of my head.

SWIPE!

Besides, wouldn't it be cool if Baskerville really was a super detective dog?

Maybe he could help us find out what's happened to the Alpine Star!

Ha ha! Fat chance! I reckon Baskerville's more interested in sniffing out dirty socks and sausages.

We were at Martha's, hanging out after school.

For ages, Sherlock had just been been sitting in a chair, staring off into space and eating those disgusting sweets of his. But now he was striding around the room, waving his arms (and my iPad) around excitedly.

"Facts, John, we must stick to the facts! And we need more of them. Although ..." he looked thoughtfully at my story again, "in some ways you're not too far off here, even if you don't realize it." Martha looked over at me and I rolled my eyes. Sherlock never just tells you what he's thinking... It can get pretty annoying sometimes, but who knows what's going on in that head?

One thing was certain; I wasn't getting my iPad back any time soon.

"Yes. There's something to be said for the merits of a good dog in clue-hunting and problem-solving," said Sherlock. "Like the time somebody locked Mr Phelps in the computer cupboard, then piled all the tables up outside the door, just for good measure."

"Ha ha! Yeah, I remember that," Martha interrupted. "It was so funny!"

"Mr Phelps went totally bonkers, banging on the door for a good half an hour, but no one could hear him. All the teachers knew he was missing but no one could find him."

"So ... what's Baskerville got to do with that then?" I said.

"It turned out that Moriarty and his chums had locked him in there.

"I had Baskerville get the scent of custard creams from the tin in the staffroom – knowing that Mr Phelps was a big fan – and he sniffed his way to the cupboard in no time!

"But never mind that, John – the point is that just thinking about Baskerville has given me a brilliant idea! You don't need to go home yet, do you? No? Good. Because we're going back to school. It's nearly time for walkies!"

I had ***no clue*** what this brilliant idea of his was, and I didn't know how it could have anything to do with Baskerville or the Alpine Star. But I don't think I need to tell you that nothing is ever obvious with Sherlock.

Luckily, Sherlock's plans for later that evening didn't involve locking teachers in cupboards. But unluckily for me, they weren't much better. And apparently we did need some custard creams...

ASK BASKERVILLE!

OK, readers! Any time there's a stinker of a problem, you need help from the best nose in town. (Or school, in this case.) So today we're going to see if we can get some help from our favourite furry chum, Baskerville.

So, Baskerville, what do you say? You wanna help us?

OK, great! That's one woof for yes. Well, then, let's get start –

WOOF! WOOF!

Oh, hang on! That's two woofs for no ... so it's not a yes, after all? Well, that must mea –

WOOF! WOOF! WOOF!

Three woofs! Well, now that's confusing. Is that a yes or a no, Baskerville, old chum?

AROOOOOOOOOO

OK, OK. And he's off!

It looks like that's all we've got time for today. That's one dog who sure NOSE what he wants! See you next time, readers!

MS. DEROSS[illegible] OFFICE

"Err... Do you really think we should be doing this?"

That was all I could think as we were scrabbling through the window in the dark. I mean, you don't need to be a brainiac to know that it wasn't a good idea to be sneaking around in school after hours...

AT ALL.

And I absolutely, definitely didn't think it was a good idea to be sneaking around in Ms DeRossi's office...

To be honest though those were the sorts of questions I should've asked myself earlier. Before I joined Baker Street Academy. Those were the sort of questions I would've asked myself before I met Sherlock Holmes. A bit late for that now!

"Really, John. There's no need for ants in your pants," said Sherlock, full of confidence. "The window was already open, wasn't it? And the caretaker, Mr Musgrave, takes Baskerville for his walk now so the coast is clear."

"Well, I think it's crazy!" At least Martha agreed with me... "But I like it! What are we looking for anyway? And why Ms DeRossi's office?" she asked as we swung our torch beams around the room.

"Well, actually there's something I didn't tell you two before..." Sherlock was already busy rummaging around Ms DeRossi's desk. "When the alarm went off at the museum and I slipped through the fire exit door, someone had gone through just ahead of me. And that person was..."

"Ms DeRossi!" gasped Martha.

""What?" I pointed my torch over to Sherlock. "Are you saying that Ms DeRossi is mixed up in trying to pinch the Alpine Star? Wait a minute – are we looking for the real jewel? In Ms DeRossi's office?!"

"Ha! Don't be silly, John... At least I don't think we are anyway."

"But—"

"We're looking for anything of interest. Anything that can help us start piecing things together. Like this! Yes! And most definitely this! Not exactly what I was expecting, but definitely what I would call suggestive!"

"What? What have you found?" Martha was getting excited and I could feel the hairs stand up on the back of my neck.

Admit One
B&A
MAP.
'THE ALPINE
Ms. C. DeRossi
001003776
STATUE COURT
MIDDLE EAST
SCULPTURE
JEWELLERY *
METALWORK
PORTRAITS
VICTORIAN
PRINTS & DRAWING
PHOTOGRAPHY
MORIARTY. J
CONFIDENTIAL.
Adult with donation
Adult with donation

"Take a look for yourself," said Sherlock, shining the torch down on to the desk.

"Blimey! She really loves that exhibition," Martha said. "That's, like, thirty tickets."

"And that's not all."

"Moriarty's school file?"

"Well – he is in trouble a lot," sighed Holmes. "But look at this..."

"A staff badge. How did she...?"

"Never mind that, John. I've seen what I needed to see and we've got about five minutes to get out of here before Mr Musgrave comes back around the corner from walkies with Baskerville! Come on, Martha."

Sherlock's brain works so fast. I still wasn't sure exactly what we'd just seen, but as we skulked off into the shadows and out of the school grounds, I couldn't get one small thing out of my mind...

"Hey! Why did I need to bring the biscuits!?"

"Ha ha! That bit was my idea, John," sniggered Martha. "Well, we've got to have a snack!"

Sherlock didn't turn up at school the next day. Martha didn't seem to know where he was either, but she didn't seem too bothered about it. Typical. I was nervous about asking Ms DeRossi where he was in case my face gave anything away – but finally I did, and she just said that Sherlock wouldn't be coming in today as he was sick. She looked preoccupied as though she had bigger things on her mind, and for the second day in a row she let us watch a video instead of working.

Sick, eh? Well, he hadn't looked sick to me last night...

When I didn't hear anything from Sherlock over the weekend either I was really starting to get worried. Martha said he was probably off doing something with his brother, but that didn't make it any better. Instead she forced me to work on our Victorian project, which we had to present to the class on Monday afternoon.

By Monday morning my head was about to explode, so imagine my astonishment when Martha and I arrived at the library to do some last-minute work on our project ... only to find Sherlock sitting there waiting at a desk without a care in the world, as if we'd only just seen him five minutes ago.

Ah, Watson. Martha.

How are you both today? Let me tell you - there is nothing quite like a good bit of exercise before breakfast!

Sherlock! We've nearly worried ourselves to death. Is everything all right?

Everything is splendid! In fact, I'd say it couldn't be better. I've been doing some digging. Our Alpine Star has quite a history to it. It would seem that there have been arguments over who rightfully owns it since the very day of its discovery. It really does make for interesting reading...

Show -&- Tell

My head felt like it was going to burst. How many more times would Sherlock astonish me? I guess I should've been getting used to it!

But I didn't have long to think about it – it was time for us to present our Victorian project to the class.

Ours went down a treat. Me and Martha and Sherlock had decided to dress up like Victorians using some of the clothes that we found at Martha's house and we acted out a little scene that Sherlock had found in one of the dusty old journals in the attic, about the detective Sherinford. I was pretty sure no one else was going to do anything as cool as that. It was like being Victorian superheroes or something!

Sherlock and Martha played Victorian detectives and I played the writer of the story, telling their spine-chilling adventures. The best bit was that Martha had borrowed Baskerville for the afternoon too, so he really did get to be a detective super dog, even if it was just for five minutes!

It was fun to see how much effort everyone else had put into their projects. Martin and Henry had built an amazing model of the

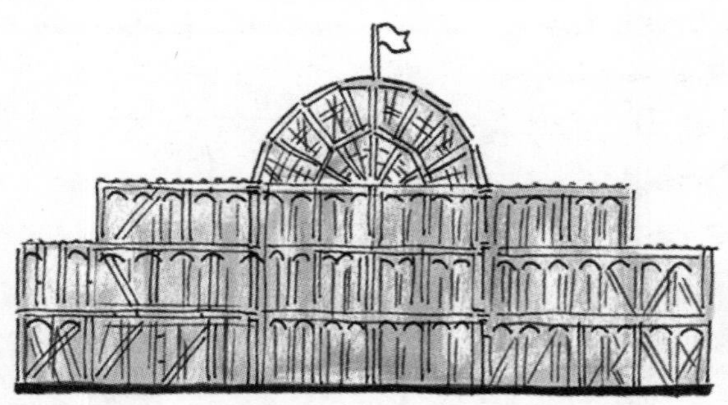

THE CRYSTAL PALACE.

Victorian Crystal Palace, like the one we'd seen at the museum, out of hundreds of wooden coffee-stirrers. It was hardly surprising it was so good. If it wasn't enough they had a police inspector dad, their mum is a genius architect!

...AND WHEN WE VISIT MUSEUMS, WE SHOULD THINK ABOUT WHO ACTUALLY OWNS THE AMAZING OBJECTS THAT WE'RE LOOKING AT. MANY OF THEM HAVE BEEN STOLEN OR TRADED OVER THE COURSE OF THEIR HISTORY. WAR AND GREED, LIES AND DECEIT HAVE OFTEN PLAYED A PART. HISTORY NEVER QUESTIONS THE WINNERS, OF COURSE, AND IT'S VERY DIFFICULT FOR THE OWNERS TO GET THEIR PROPERTY BACK.
TAKE THE ANCIENT MARBLES, OR THE ROMAN PILLARS FOR EXAMPLE.
OR EVEN SIMPLE FAMILY HEIRLOOMS LIKE THE GELDER NAPOLEONS...

But the biggest surprise of all was James's presentation. It was about why museums get to keep objects belonging to other countries. For once he seemed really serious and not at all snarky.

...THERE ARE STILL PEOPLE WHO QUESTION THE OWNERSHIP OF SOME OF OUR MOST TREASURED ITEMS LIKE THE ALPINE STAR AND WANT TO SEE THESE PRECIOUS ARTEFACTS RETURNED TO THEIR ... RIGHTFUL OWNERS. IT'S AMAZING WHAT LENGTHS SOME PEOPLE WILL GO TO IN ORDER TO MAKE SURE THEY GET ARTEFACTS BACK. THE TROUBLE IS THAT MUSEUMS ARE FILLED WITH PEOPLE WHO WILL INSIST ON INTERFERING IN OTHER PEOPLE'S BUSINESS. DON'T YOU THINK SO, SHERLOCK?

"This is actually pretty good," I whispered to Sherlock. "Hey, isn't that the same statue of Napoleon that I drew that day at the museum, before the Alpine Star went missing?"

"Yes, it is, John. Yes, it is." Sherlock said thoughtfully.

I have to admit that it was really interesting! Ms DeRossi was impressed too, I could tell – she was staring at James open-mouthed. It was a shame that James just couldn't resist a dig at Sherlock though. Something bad's going to happen with them soon, I just know it. Not that Sherlock looked too bothered. In fact he had one of those looks on his face and I knew that his megabrain was clicking into gear...

BREAKING NEWS!

We were all milling about in the corridor after class when Sherlock's pocket started buzzing.

"How very interesting!" he said quietly, showing me his phone. "Don't you think so, John?"

It was a text message – I assume from his brother, Mycroft.

bzZzZzt
bzZzZzt
11:08
Message now
Pietro Vencini is being released this afternoon. M
Slide to view

"Interesting?! I'd say so. Pietro Vencini is the—"

"Precisely, John. The thief."

Sherlock was tapping away furiously. Finally he clicked to the news website. The almost-thief, Pietro Vencini, was all over it again.

"Look," I said, "Mycroft was right. There's a video here of him being released."

"'New evidence has come to light.' And he's given a statement too:"

I AM VERY MUCH LOOKING FORWARD TO GOING BACK TO THE MUSEUM. AND SEEING MY LITTLE DOG, NAPOLEON. AND MY WIFE, OF COURSE. THANK YOU.

Weird. Didn't he say something like that before? Who calls their dog Napoleon?

og? I thought it was his son?

Ha! That's it - oh, that's brilliant. A very clever plan. Even I have to admit it. Yes, it all makes sense now. But we have definitely got to get our skates on. You haven't got any plans after school now, have you? Good. Oh you do? Well - cancel them. And Martha, I need you to do something for me, if you don't mind? Come on, John, don't just sit there...

So, like I said, I don't mind a bit of adventure...

There IS a gate, Sherlock!

No time for that, Watson. In fact we've got about sixty seconds ....

But how much adventure can one kid take?

10 THE CHASE IS ON!

Sixty seconds?!
Yes. Just around this corner now. I hope we're still in time!
For what?!
The number 74 bus, John.
How else are we going to get to the museum?
74 BACK TO THE MUSEUM

AN ADVENTURE WITH NAPOLEON

And that bit about him being like a bloodhound on a scent? I was right about that too.

Sherlock didn't say a word once we had leapt on to the bus. It was like he was in a trance, that megabrain of his whirring away. But suddenly, as the museum came into view, he sprang to life. He jumped off the bus and I had to sprint to keep up with him.

"What are we doing, Sherlock?" I panted. "Shouldn't we be leaving this stuff to the police?" I knew he was hot on the trail of something massively important, but I couldn't help thinking we should be getting a bit of help!

As we approached the giant steps up to the entrance, I thought I could make out a familiar figure going in through the doors ahead of us.

"Wait a minute, Sherlock. Is that James Moriarty?" Now things were getting confusing. What on earth was James Moriarty doing here? And what was Sherlock doing chasing after him?

With my thoughts racing, my blood pumping and the sounds of the busy

London streets in my ears I thought I could make out the ever-closer siren of a police car...

Sherlock flung himself through the museum entrance doors and I puffed along after him. It was nearly closing time so it wasn't that busy, but that didn't stop me losing sight of him almost immediately.

"Sherlock!" I tore after him, scattering a few end-of-day stragglers and tourists doing the rounds.

As I rushed through the maze of pillars and statues, I lost sight of him. I sprinted up the nearest set of big marble stairs to the gallery above, so that I could look down on the sculpture room and hopefully catch a glimpse of him.

Just then a voice echoed up from the vast space below...

YOU JUST CAN'T LEAVE THINGS ALONE, CAN YOU, SHERLOCK? ALWAYS SNOOPING. ALWAYS STICKING YOUR STUPID NOSE IN WHERE IT DOESN'T BELONG.

There was no mistaking it this time. It was definitely James Moriarty. I hadn't been seeing things!

I finally caught sight of Sherlock below. He'd come in through one entrance just as Moriarty was coming in the other. "You're one to talk, James," replied Sherlock from the other side of the room. "I'm just interested in things. And you will keep making yourself so very … interesting." I couldn't believe what I was seeing. It was like some sort of crazy wild-west stand-off, with the two of them waiting to see who would draw first.

I pulled myself together and turned back down the stairs. As I ran, I could hear Moriarty shouting:

LOOK AT YOU, SHERLOCK! THE ANNOYING ITCH THAT JUST WON'T GO AWAY. I'VE HAD JUST ABOUT ENOUGH OF YOU GETTING IN THE WAY ALL THE TIME. I'M GETTING THE REICHENBACH JEWEL BACK WHETHER YOU LIKE IT OR NOT.

"Really, James. I wouldn't do that if I were you..." exclaimed Sherlock.

I burst through the doors into the sculpture room. They were slowly circling each other now, in and out around the bases of the pillars and statues. As I made my way towards them...

"Stay out of it, Sherlock," warned Moriarty. "I'm only trying to get back what's rightfully mine!"

"Wrongfully yours is a more fitting description."

I had no idea what Moriarty was talking about. The Reichenbach Jewel?

What was that? Rightfully his? What on earth was going on? Sherlock and James looked at each other in silence. I could feel the tension in the air...

As I got closer, I could see James edging closer to a group of statues. Sherlock laughed. "Oh, I know what you're doing, Moriarty. We both figured out those messages, didn't we? The family man..." Sherlock nodded towards a statue of a man holding two small children, "And of course, Napoleon, pointing at a pillar..."

Moriarty suddenly broke away to one side of the room. He ran at the statue of a man holding two children and then jumped up on to the low plinth of the figure right next to it. Desperately, he began to climb the giant figure. And that's when I noticed that it was a statue of Napoleon, his arm outstretched.

"Don't do it, James. Get down! The police will be here any minute now. You'll only make things worse for yourself."

"Shut up, Sherlock!"

Just then, the alarms started to go off around us and I stopped dead in my tracks. It was like the flash mob all over again! James Moriarty had nearly scaled the figure. Balancing on his shoulders he reached up to the French Emperor's hat...

"Yes! I knew it!" he shouted. "I've got it! Now you know to stay out of my business, Sherlock. It's time to restore a bit of family heritage..."

As he pulled his hand away from the statue I could see Moriarty was clutching something tight in his hand - but it was only when the museum lights caught its surface that I realized what I was seeing... James Moriarty had got the Alpine Star!

INSPECTOR
BAKER
CALLS
11

I was totally dumbstruck.

But just as I thought things couldn't get any stranger, out of the shadows sprang our not-so-innocent museum thief, Pietro Vencini. He shot in front of me, past Sherlock and bounded up on to the base of the Napoleon statue alongside Moriarty.

"If you please, Signor Moriarty." His voice

was cold and commanding. "I will take that Reichenbach Jewel. You would not want to upset the professor once more." Pietro had a sinister look on his face and you could tell he meant every word.

It was cat and mouse for a split second, but Pietro was a tall man and it was easy for him to snatch the gleaming jewel from James's grasp and jump back down from the base of the statue.

"No!" shouted Moriarty,

scrambling down after Vencini. "You've already messed it up once! It's mine and I want to take it home where it belongs."

He lunged after Vencini, but Sherlock threw out an arm to block him. "James, stop!"

"Get off me, you meddler."

"No, really, in a few seconds I think you will agree with me that you'd better leave this one alone. In just a few seconds..."

Moriarty stuttered and Pietro backed away, smiling grimly. "You will thank me later, Signor James."

Then he ran for the door... But he didn't get more than the length of the room before he was blocked at all exits by police officers, a serious-looking DI Baker and ...

MARTHA?!

And, wait a minute ...

MS DEROSSI?!

I felt like I'd been holding my breath for ever but suddenly the life burst back into me.

"Ms DeRossi! Martha? What are you doing here?" I spluttered. "Detective Inspector Baker... Sherlock, what's going on?"

"Don't worry, John. I asked Martha to rally the troops and meet us here. I think you could say that everything is safely 'in hand'." Sherlock had a gleam in his eye and a wide smile on his face.

"Ah, good afternoon, Detective Inspector Baker. John, allow me to introduce you to Ms Carla DeRossi, senior representative in the Italian Antiquities Agency, and quite possibly one of the best intelligence agents that the Metropolitan Police could wish for in an arts-related criminal inquiry such as this."

Ms DeRossi nodded to me and then turned her attention to the wriggling Vencini who was red-faced with rage.

What?! I just couldn't believe what I was hearing!

MS DEROSSI WAS A DETECTIVE TOO?

Talk about brain-busting! With all the excitement, my glasses had steamed up. So typical of Sherlock to spring it all on us right at the end, after we've been flopping around like fishes out of water for so long. Sometimes it would be nice to actually know what's going on!

Meanwhile Moriarty was slumped at the base of the Napoleon statue, muttering furiously. "We're not finished you know, Sherlock. Not by a long shot. You and your pathetic little followers... You've got no idea what's it's like to walk in the shadow of a surname like mine..."

For a moment I felt pretty sorry for him, but there was no time for that as Detective Inspector Baker coolly slapped a pair of handcuffs on Pietro Vencini and brought the priceless diamond over to Ms DeRossi.

"I think this would be safer in your hands for the time being, Ms DeRossi. Our friend Mr Vencini certainly won't be needing it any time soon. I think there'll be a few questions asked about exactly how all of you kids came to be involved in this business though, especially you, young Mr Moriarty. But I'd say we've had enough excitement for one afternoon."

"Thank you, Detective Inspector Baker," said Ms DeRossi. "I agree - and in future I'd rather you were all safely in school instead of chasing jewels and criminals around. That's a job best left to the police! The important thing is that the museum will be extremely grateful for the safe return of their troublesome diamond. I should think they would like to add their thanks to you too, Sherlock. Well done. And now," she smiled, "perhaps you would like to see what all the fuss was about."

Ms DeRossi held up the diamond for us all to see. It gleamed and sparkled brilliantly under the museum lights, just like a star.

"Wow!" said Martha.

"It really is amazing, isn't it? I can't believe something so small has caused all this fuss though."

"Yeah! Tell me about it! I can't believe that our teacher was working with the police, and that Sherlock knew about it too!"

The Reichenbach Jewel

"I'm not sure I understand it all properly though," I said to Sherlock as Ms DeRossi escorted James away and several police officers dragged the struggling and cursing Vencini from the museum. "Is the Reichenbach Jewel the same as the Alpine Star? And who's this 'professor' guy?"

"The 'professor guy' is James's father – a brilliant and dangerous criminal called Professor Moriarty. And as for the diamonds, the truth is that they're one and the same, Watson – but it wasn't until I did some digging with the help of Mycroft that I realized quite how involved the Moriarty family actually were.

"You see, to the Moriarty family, it was never the Alpine Star at all. To them it is the Reichenbach Jewel, a long-lost family treasure, stolen from them well over a century ago.

Prof. MORIARTY.

"In 1887, Professor Moriarty, James's great-great-great-grandfather, was part of an expedition party who found the priceless diamond. But there were confrontations and disagreements from the very moment it was pulled from the ground, not to mention murder and deceit. It resulted in the professor being expelled from the group and his name was scrubbed from the official records. But the professor had hereditary tendencies of the most diabolical kind, John. A criminal strain ran through his blood. He retreated to his hideaway in Switzerland, near the famous Reichenbach Falls, swearing revenge on those who had wronged him! He was known as the Napoleon of crime."

"Oh! Napoleon. Like the statue," I said. "And the Reichenbach Falls – like the jewel!" At least that bit made sense now.

It's really quite simple when you look at all the pieces. You see, John, unlike the rest of the world, I was certain that the Star had indeed been stolen on the day of our visit to the museum. I've seen the Alpine Star many times before and I knew that the jewel that had been on display was the genuine article. It had distinct features that the fake - although brilliant in itself - did not possess. I made sure of that when we went back to look at it. From there I just had to work my way through the clues...
I knew that James was up to no good from the

rst time we visited the museum - I'd seen him talking with Vencini earlier, and he was the only one who didn't turn to look at the flash mob, so I lecided to keep an eye on him. And after realizing that the Moriarty family had a connection to the whole affair, I could make better sense of the events at the museum.

The Professor's plan was that Mr Pietro Vencini, masquerading as a member of the museum staff, would arrive at the museum with a fake jewel. At a certain time, there would be a distracting incident in one of the display rooms - the flash mob, paid to cause a scene. Once the confusion and craziness was in full effect, Pietro would steal the real ewel and hand it to an accomplice, keeping the fake with him. He always intended to be caught, you see.

"The thief, Pietro, would then make a very public getaway with the fake jewel in his possession, only to be easily caught by the police. Perhaps too easily... Later the fake would be exposed, causing outrage all around the world, discrediting the museum and leaving the real jewel in the hands of the mastermind behind the whole plan – in this case, almost certainly James's father, the current Professor Moriarty. Although I think both the police and Ms DeRossi would have a hard time proving any criminal link other than the family history I told you about already, John..."

"Blimey! No wonder James is so snarky all the time," said Martha. "It must be pretty hard when you've got a family tree like that."

"Exactly right, Martha," agreed Sherlock. "The apple does not fall far from the tree!"

"That's a good plan," I admitted. "Vencini was clearly hoping his associates would decode the message and return to collect the real jewel that was hidden on the statue of Napoleon..."

"...On the pillar," Martha said. "And pointing."

Exactly right again. But one thing went wrong... Ms DeRossi, our fabulous agent from Italy, had her own suspicions that something strange would be happening at the museum. She had been tracking Mr Vencini for some time, and it's no coincidence that she organized a school trip to the B&A that day. It gave her the perfect cover. She had an idea of who the accomplice would be and when the flash mob started she followed them closely to observe the planned handover of the real jewel from the thief.

But who was this mystery accomplice?

I'm afraid it was young James Moriarty. And he made a foolish mistake getting involved in his father's affairs - he panicked when he saw Ms DeRossi was following him and missed the moment of handover, meaning that Vencini found himself with both the real and the fake jewels on his person.
Pietro had to make a run for it - first hiding the jewel in Napoleon's hat, sure that he could retrieve it later or tell the Professor where it was hidden.
And it wasn't till I had made sense of the ridiculous statements that Vencini's lawyer kept putting out that I realized the Alpine Star had been right under our noses - or should I say hats - all along! Remember, John...

This is what Vencini said:

"My client is a kind-hearted family man, a devoted husband to his wife and little Napoleon.

All this points to him being an upstanding pillar of the community. He has nothing to hide under his hat and he is very much hoping to be able to return to the museum shortly."

Is it getting any clearer, John?

I looked around at the statues next to us and it all started to make sense. "Oh, yeah! I get it now... The kind-hearted family man... And Napoleon, pointing up at the pillar...That's cool!"

"Indeed. The message could not have been clearer. But as it turns out, the only person to decode it was our friend James Moriarty. And me, of course." Sherlock exclaimed.

"That's brilliant, Sherlock! I mean, I know I've said it before, like a hundred times or something, but really, the whole thing is just amazing. The way you've pieced it all together and figured it out... Just brilliant."

"Yeah, I have to agree with John this time, Sherlock," nodded Martha. "It has been pretty amazing. Even for a big head like you! Haha!"

"One last thing though," I said. "How did you know that Ms DeRossi was one of the good guys? You had us thinking that she was involved in the theft."

"Well, she was, of course, John, just not in the way you and Martha were thinking! It was

obvious from all the tickets we found in her office during our little after-hours 'study session' that she had been to the museum many times. She had also gone to the trouble of obtaining a staff badge so that she could go about the museum undisturbed. She had clearly been researching the history of the Alpine Star and had discovered the connection to the Moriarty family - she had old newspaper reports on her desk as well as Moriarty's file. Finally, there was a connection with DI Baker, and I found the correspondence to confirm it.

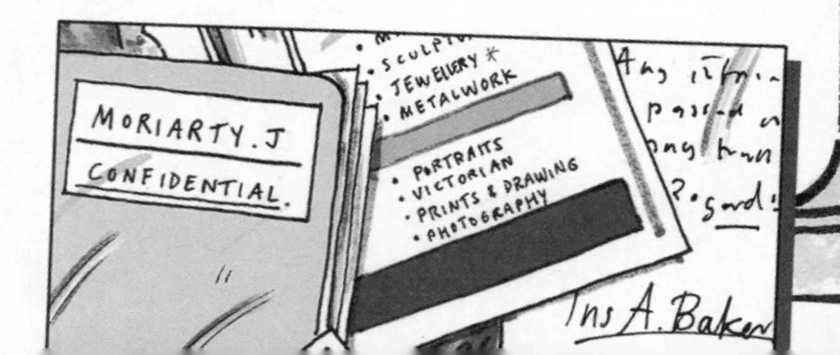

But sometimes I like to watch you both come to your own conclusions, you know... It makes it all so much more fun for me!"

The three of us burst out laughing as we stood there in the statue gallery room. The lights were going off and the staff and a couple of remaining police officers were waiting to see us out of the museum safely. It felt like a full stop in the adventure. I just couldn't get over how incredible the last few weeks had been. I know Sherlock thinks I get carried away, but I am definitely going to have to write about this when I get back home!

Arts Online: Ne..

https://www.artsonline.co.uk/news-museums-london-b&a-itsback-

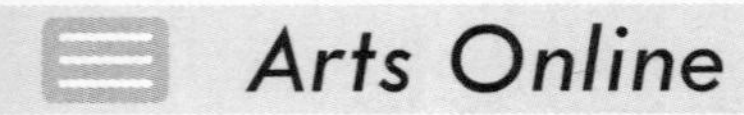

News > Museums > London

THIRD TIME LUCKY!

Well, they say that things happen in threes and it certainly looks like it's third time lucky for the B&A museum now that they've actually managed to get their hands back on the Alpine Star. Click here for the full story.

SCHOOLBOY SAVES MUSEUM'S BLUSHES

ALPINE STAR BUNGLER FOILED AGAIN!

PRICELESS DIAMOND FOUND SAFE AT MUSEUM

As usual our crazy escapades ended up with us all hanging out back at 221B Baker Street. Only this time we had an extra member of the gang, because Baskerville had come to join the fun! Martha and her mum were looking after him while Mr and Mrs Musgrave were away for the holidays.

Sherlock was particularly happy, as it turned out that he was going to be staying at 221B from now on too! Mycroft was going to university and would be away for most of the year (I reckon he's actually off somewhere top-secret!).

Sherlock's amazing revelations had made the news, and he was quickly becoming the "star" of Baker Street

Academy, with just about everybody wanting to know how he managed to work it all out. The museum mystery really did seem simple when he explained it in his own Sherlock way, but that didn't spoil it for me at all. I still think the whole thing was amazing - and it was crazy to think that the real diamond was there under our noses all the time! The B&A gave us membership passes so we could go and see the exhibitions as often as we wanted, which was so cool. I just couldn't wait to go back. And Detective Baker invited us in to see the police commissioner and get a special award. Yep. Life was great and everything felt good.

But there was one thing that was still bothering me, and I just couldn't resist asking Sherlock: "How did you know all that stuff about me when we first met?"

"Ha, ha! That's still bugging you is it, John?" He and Martha were both laughing. "All right then," he said, "but if I keep telling you my little observations, it's all going to seem so simple! Let's start with your name, shall we?

"When you came into the science lab with Martha, I could clearly see your surname and initial on the airport flight tag still hanging from your bag. I tried James for the J, but the look in your eyes instantly said no and I was right with John on the second try. From there it was easy to see you'd just recently got back from abroad..."

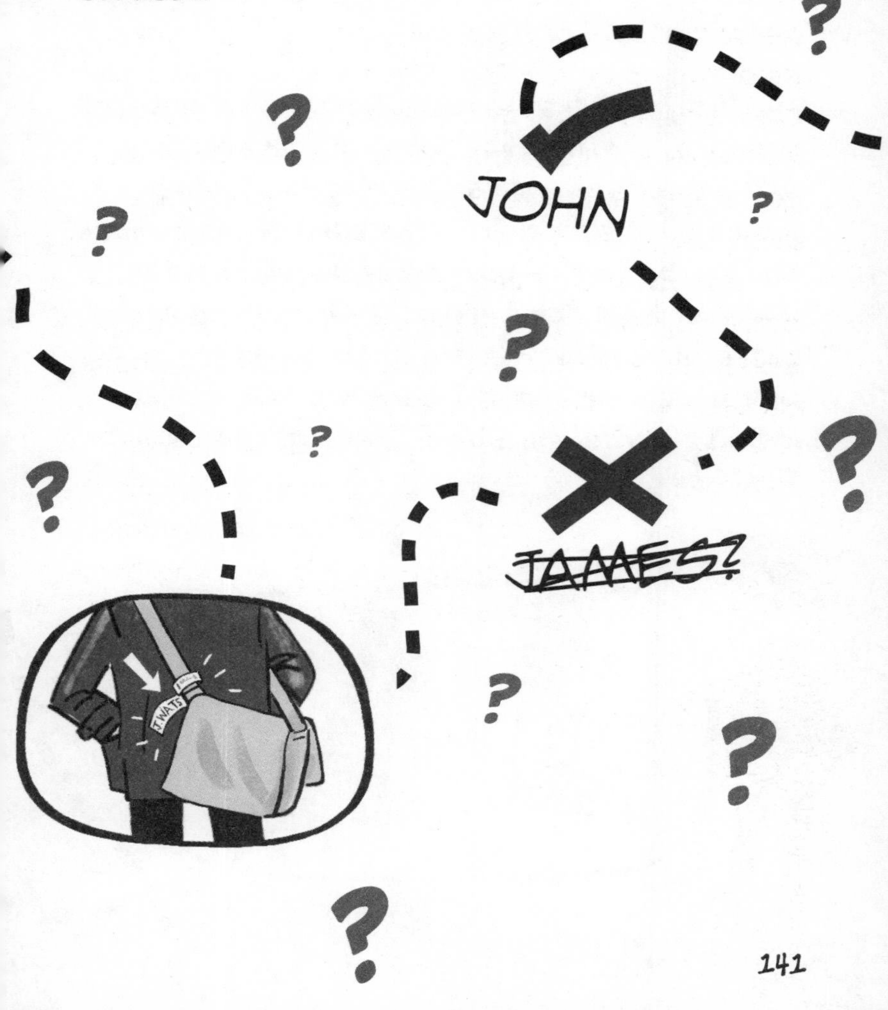

"Your fingers were stained with ink or pencil smudges, showing that you wrote or sketched. And I could tell you had had trouble finding your way to school from the sand on your shoes and the bottom of your trousers, which meant you must have come from the side of the school where the roadworks are at the moment. Is that enough or should I carry on? Oh, you're lost for words, eh, John? That's got to be a first for you.

"The other bits were so obvious, even Baskerville could have pointed them out. The hot-chocolate splashes and the croissant flakes, not to mention the custard creams packet that was half sticking out of your coat pocket. You were like a walking snack shop!"

I was too stunned to speak. Luckily, as if by magic, Mrs Hudson came in with the biggest tray of snacks and hot chocolate I'd ever seen!

Look at the three of you! Proper little detectives now, aren't you?
Oh yes, you too, Baskerville, he-heh!
WOOF!
What are your plans for the holidays then, John? Will you go somewhere with your parents?
I don't think so, Mrs Hudson. I'm not sure yet, but it looks like Mum and Dad might be called away for work, so I don't know where I'll be actually!
What? No way! That's no good, John. You'll miss all the fun. You should come and stay here with us!
Mum, can he stay with us? He can, can't he?
I couldn't think of a better suggestion, Martha.
Well, I don't know, Martha. But I could talk to your parents if you like, John? I suppose you two boys practically live here already!

LOL-mail

https://www.mail.lol.co.uk/webmail-std/en-gb/DisplayMessage?ws_pc

olMail.

Hi Son!

From: Mummy

To: Watson, John

Tuesday 17th,

Hello, John,

Just a quick message to let you know that your dad and I have arrived safely at the Medical Base Camp. Phone contact might be a bit patchy to start with – but hopefully this will be a straightforward trip and we'll be back before you've even had a chance to miss us!
In the meantime, we're sure Mrs Hudson is going to take very good care of you, but even more sure you'll have an amazing time with your friends. You deserve a good fun-filled break!
We'll be in touch as soon as we can, OK, sweetie.

Love from Mum & Dad x x

So there you have it. That's me: John Watson, the not-so-new boy at Baker Street Academy, and that was the end of my first adventure. Pretty cool, huh? I've met some amazing people and made some even more amazing friends. And, oh yeah, I've met Sherlock Holmes.

I'm going to miss not having Mum and Dad around for the next few months, although staying at 221B with Mrs Hudson and Martha and Sherlock and Baskerville will be awesome! Living just down the street from school means I get to lie-in every day. And I'll have all of London at my door. Whoop! It's going to be so cool, I just can't wait!

THE END?

Seeing as there's room for it, I'd like to say a big thank you, no, actually a HUGE thank you to the team at Scholastic UK. For over a year, they helped me first find my feet and then allowed me to cut loose on this amazing, dream job of a project.

Andrew Biscomb, Samantha Smith, Genevieve Herr and Liam Drane have all been incredibly encouraging and supportive from day one. Special mention goes to Emily Lamm, who put up with me for months and gave me the confidence to turn all my ideas into something resembling a story.

Thanks to Jamie at Elephant & Bird for loads of things, not least letting me be part of the workplace and feel like I'm

From SAM HEARN

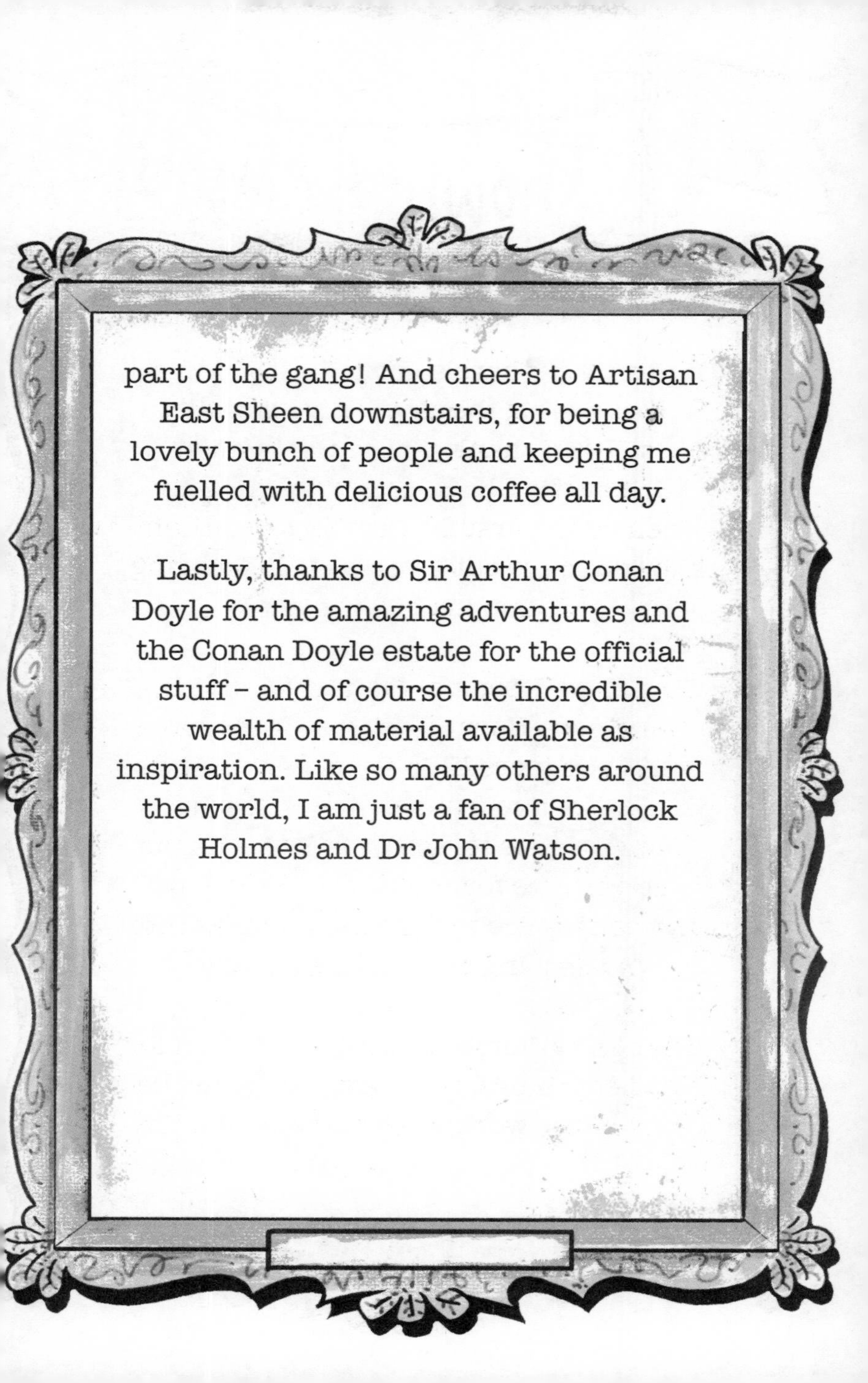

part of the gang! And cheers to Artisan East Sheen downstairs, for being a lovely bunch of people and keeping me fuelled with delicious coffee all day.

Lastly, thanks to Sir Arthur Conan Doyle for the amazing adventures and the Conan Doyle estate for the official stuff – and of course the incredible wealth of material available as inspiration. Like so many others around the world, I am just a fan of Sherlock Holmes and Dr John Watson.

Here's a gallery of some of the very first drawings Sam did, before starting work on the full project.

SAM HEARN

SAM HEARN

SAM HEARN

JUST WHO IS SAM HEARN?

No one that I've asked seems to know much about this suspicious character. Perhaps that's deliberate, but I can't be sure...

I've done a bit of digging, and from my investigations, it looks like he's been interfering with other people's books for over 15 years!

What I can say is, it definitely feels like someone has been following us around ever since I arrived at Baker Street Academy... Martha's not happy about it at all - and Sherlock is suspicious of anybody claiming to use the same initials as him. All very suspect if you ask me! I'll let you know if I find out anything else.